Printed in the United States of America

www.frontpagepublishing.com

Front Page Publishing, LLC
5198 Arlington Ave., Suite 335
Riverside, CA 92504

This book is dedicated to my son & his family Samuel Dennis, Brittani and Ethan

Everybody freeze. Don't move. Don't laugh.
Justin's tooth fell out, and it's in this class.

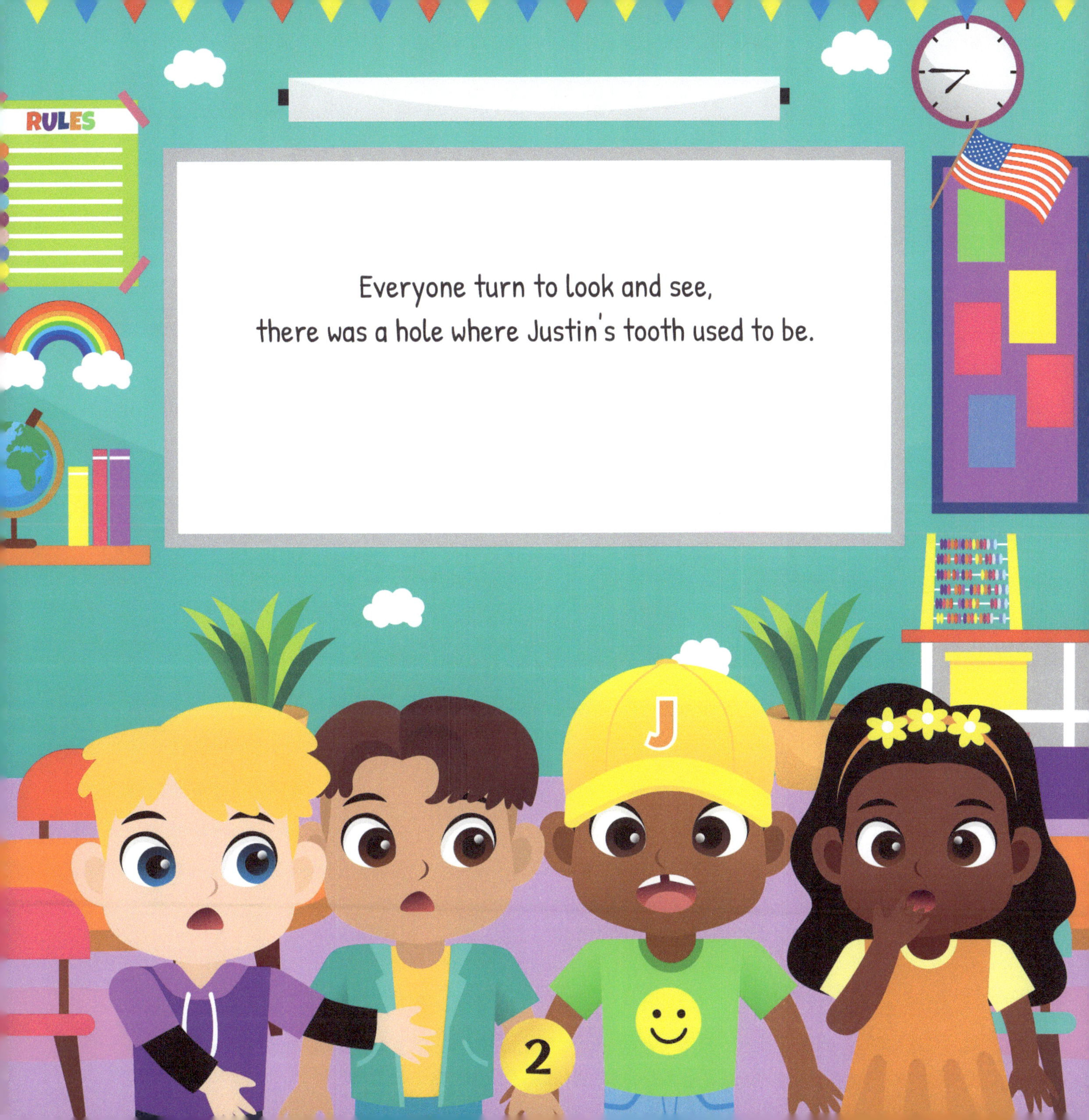

Everyone turn to look and see,
there was a hole where Justin's tooth used to be.

J
This was serious business
and we all knew
Justin needs his tooth
for the tooth fairy
to come soon.
3

You place your tooth under your pillow
and lo' and behold.
In the morning The Tooth Fairy
leaves you money, some silver...some gold.

The question is,
now what to do?
We can't stay frozen
the whole day through!

"Down on your knees", was Justin's next command.
We all understood the emergency. The Tooth Fairy comes by after your tooth comes out, you see!

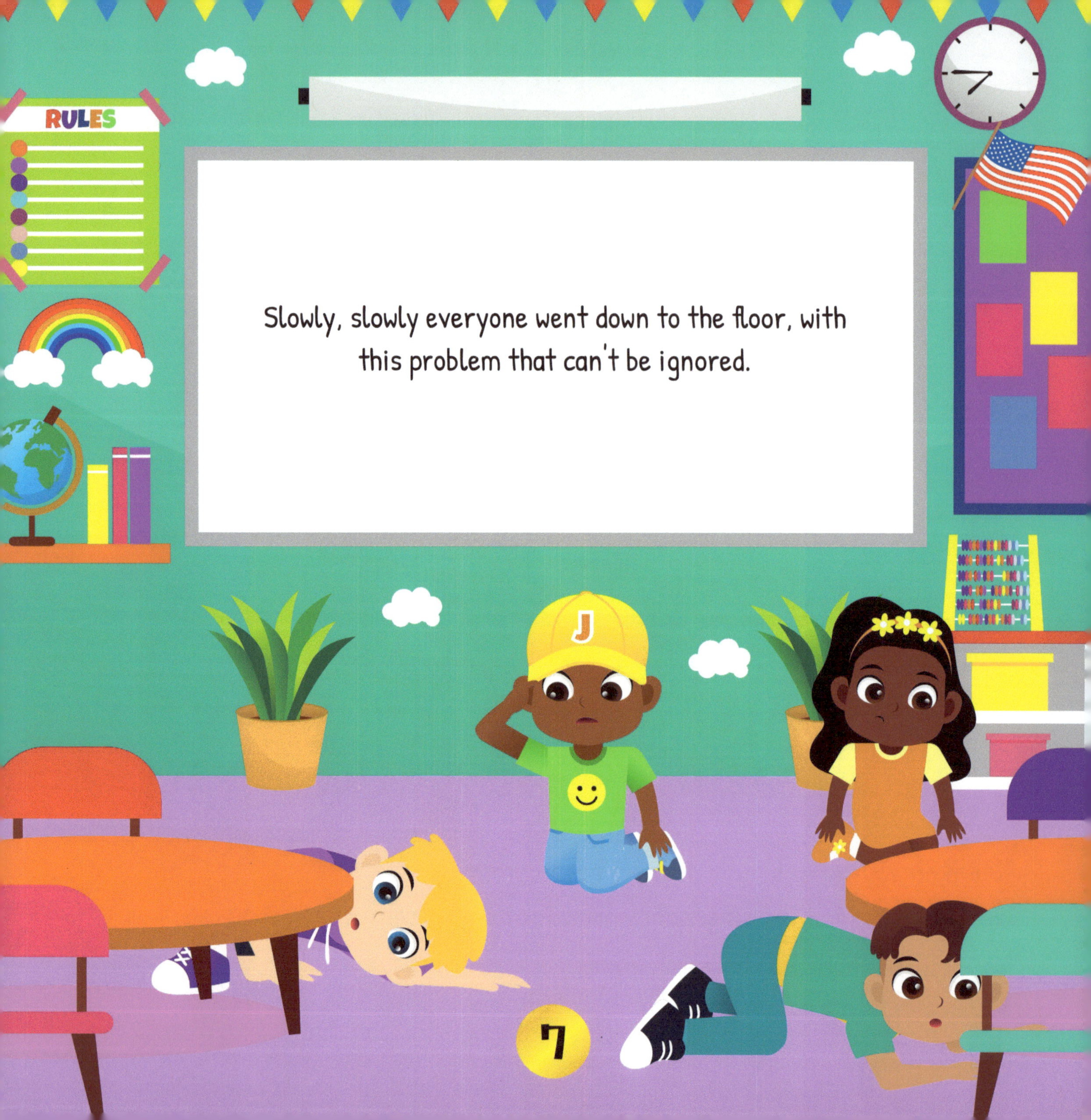

Slowly, slowly everyone went down to the floor, with this problem that can't be ignored.

We could hear the sadness in Justin's voice, "Do you feel anything on the floor, anything at all? Anything that feels like a tooth, anything that small?"

Ms. Stokes had been quiet, but now she began,
"Justin, just when did you notice your tooth wasn't in?"

WAS IT AT RECESS?

WAS IT DURING NAP TIME?

WAS IT AT LUNCH OR BEFORE?

When was the last time you wiggled your tooth?
"You have been doing your work so diligently. I
didn't notice your tooth was missing, you see!"

Justin began, the class was
completely quiet while he spoke.
"I was sitting at my desk, my
work was almost complete.
Then I felt a hole where my tooth
used to be.
I was surprised because there was
no warning."

Using my tongue to push my tooth, but this time there was nothing there...my tongue was only pushing air!

"There it is, there it is," Armando said!
The tooth was in Justin's book.
Everyone turned to look and see,
Justin's tooth was right where Armando
said it would be!

The mystery was solved and back to work they would go.

Justin put his tooth under his pillow.

BASEBALL
That night as he slept
the Tooth Fairy came, she exchanged his
tooth for money as he would later proclaim.

My friends all helped and Ms. Stokes too!
Finding my missing tooth was one of the best
things they all helped me to do!

www.ingramcontent.com/pod-product-compliance
Lightning Source LLC
Chambersburg PA
CBHW041359010726
47507CB00002B/215

* 9 7 8 1 9 5 1 7 0 5 2 6 8 *